D0460715

THE DINOSAUR THAT
POOPED
CHRISTMAS!

CHECK OUT DANNY AND DINOSAUR IN MORE ADVENTURES:

THE DINOSAUR THAT POOPED A PLANET!

THE DINOSAUR THAT POOPED THE PAST!

THE DINOSAUR THAT POOPED THE BED!

For Dougie, from Tom
For Tom, from Dougie

ALADDIN

An imprint of Simon & Schuster Children's Publishing Division

1230 Avenue of the Americas, New York, New York 10020

This Aladdin hardcover edition September 2019

Illustrations by Garry Parsons

Originally published in Great Britain by Red Fox.

Published by arrangement with Penguin Random House Children's UK

Manufactured in China 0521 SCP

10 9 8 7 6 5 4 3

Library of Congress Control Number 2018959719

ISBN 978-1-4814-9872-2 (hc)

ISBN 978-1-4814-9873-9 (eBook)

THE DINOSAUR THAT POOPED CHRISTMAS!

Tom Fletcher & Dougie Poynter
Illustrated by Garry Parsons

ALADDIN
NEW YORK LONDON TORONTO SYDNEY NEW DELHI

From high in the sky Santa looked down below
To houses all cozy and covered in snow,
Where snoozers were snoozing, tucked up in their beds
While dreaming the most festive dreams in their heads.

But one boy named Danny was greedy, you see,
At least ten times greedier than good boys should be.
He lay wide awake on his mountain of toys,
Which stood even taller than most girls and boys.

But that wasn't enough—Danny still wanted more.
He wanted much more than his toy box could store.

So big Santy C said, "I'll leave him a present,
But this year his present might just be unpleasant."

Danny heard
such a clatter,
his heart skipped
a thump—
'Twas the clopping
of hooves going
clippety-clump.

He bounced out of bed and threw on some clothes

And crept
down the stairs
on his tip-tippy-toes.

There, under the tree, were gifts big and small
And a **GIGANTIC**
egg placed in front of them all.

"Santa brought me an egg? An *egg*?!" Danny said.

Then out with a

CRACK!

popped a dinosaur's head!

It wasted no time on that cold Christmas morning
And started to eat everything without warning.

It swallowed the stockings and Christmas cards too,
The red fairy lights, then the green and the blue.
There wasn't a single thing Danny could do,
Except sit and watch the dinosaur chew.

It chewed and it munched and it crunched on Kris Kringle,
The reindeer, the sleigh bells, and all things that jingle.

But it didn't stop there—there were more things to gobble,
Much more than the small shiny baubles that bobble.

It ate up the cat and the dog and the fish,
And from the dishwasher it downed every dish.
The tables, the chairs, the walls, and the doors—
Now nothing was safe, not even the floors.

Now, Reader,
BEWARE,
the next part is scary,
And if you read on,
you'll need new underwear-y.

Knitting some socks was Danny's sweet gran,
Who had no idea of the dinosaur's plan.

It slurped her right up—and the socks she was knitting
Along with the couch where she always liked sitting.

Then it ate Danny's mom—
she was gone in one bite—
And the dino was now double
Danny's dad's height.

So with no point in him
even trying to fight,
He leapt in its mouth,
wishing all a good night!

Now nothing was left—
all Danny could see
Was a fat dinosaur
where his home used to be.

But it wasn't the house
or the presents he missed;
Without *family*,
Christmas just doesn't exist.

With the feeling of guilt
in the dinosaur's gut,

Its brain brewed a plan
involving its butt.

It knew there was only one thing it could do:
To make Christmas right, it needed to . . .

POO!

It pooped out the turkey and toys from its belly,
And even the tinsel was now brown and smelly.
It pooped all the presents and pieces of puzzles.
It pooped all the things it had previously guzzled.
And then Father Christmas yelled, "OUT OF THE WAY!"
As he flew from the dinosaur's butt on his sleigh.

The dinosaur finally gave a huge push
And pooped Danny's parents in one massive

WHOOOOOOOSH!

Last to plop out was Gran
with her knitting,
Still sat on the couch where she
always liked sitting.

“Merry Christmas,” said Dan to his whole family
As they washed off the presents and put up the tree.
And the greedy young kid who you saw just before
Promised next Christmas he’d not ask for more.

And the dinosaur
promised he'd
keep his mouth shut . . .

. . . as you would if Christmas came out of your butt!